D1487355

Editors: Ann Redpath, Etienne Delessert
Art Director: Rita Marshall

Publisher: George R. Peterson, Jr.
Copyright © 1983 Creative Education, Inc., 123 S. Broad Street,
Mankato, Minnesota 56001, USA. American Edition.
Copyright © 1983 Grasset & Fasquelle, Paris – Editions 24 Heures, Lausanne. French Edition.
International copyrights reserved in all countries.

Library of Congress Catalog Card No.: 83-71178
English Fairy Tale; Jack and the Beanstalk
Mankato, MN: Creative Education, Inc.; 32 pages. ISBN: 0-87191-947-8

Printed in Switzerland by Imprimeries Réunies S.A. Lausanne.

JACK AND THE BEANSTALK

ENGLISH FAIRY TALE
illustrated by
ANDRÉ FRANÇOIS

CREATIVE EDUCATION INC.

THERE was a poor widow who had an only son named Jack, and a cow named Milky-white. And all they had to live on was the milk the cow gave every morning, which they carried to the market and sold. But one morning Milky-white gave no milk, and they didn't know what to do.

"What shall we do, what shall we do?" said the widow, wringing her hands.

"Cheer up, mother, I'll go and get some work," said Jack.

"We've tried that before, and nobody would take you," said his mother. "We must sell Milky-white, and with the money start a shop, or something."

"All right, mother," said Jack; "it's market-day today, and I'll soon sell Milky-white. Then we'll see what we can do."

So he took the cow's halter in his hand, and off he started.

He hadn't gone far when he met a funny-looking old man, who said to him:

"Good morning, Jack."

"Good morning to you," said Jack, and wondered how he knew his name.

"Well, Jack, and where are you off to?" said the man.

"I'm going to market to sell our cow."

"Oh, you look the proper sort of chap to sell cows," said the man. "I wonder if you know how many beans make five."

"Two in each hand and one in your mouth," says Jack, as sharp as a needle.

"Right you are," says the man, "and here they are, the very beans themselves," he went on, pulling out of his pocket a number of strange-looking beans. "As you are so sharp," says he, "I don't mind doing a swap with you—your cow for these beans."

"Go along," says Jack, "wouldn't you like it?"

"Ah! you don't know what these beans are," said the man. "If you plant them over-night, by morning they grow right up to the sky."

"Really?" said Jack, "you don't say so."

"Yes, that is so, and if it doesn't turn out to be true you can have your cow back."

"Right," says Jack, and hands him over Milky-white's halter and pockets the beans.

Back goes Jack home, and as he hadn't gone very far it wasn't dusk by the time he got to his door.

"Back already, Jack?" said his mother. "I see you haven't got Milky-white, so you've sold her. How much did you get for her?"

"You'll never guess, mother," says Jack.

"No, you don't say so. Good boy! Five pounds, ten, fifteen, no, it can't be twenty."

"I told you you couldn't guess. What do you say to these beans; they're magical, plant them overnight and—"

"What!" says Jack's mother, "have you been such a fool, such a dolt, such an idiot, as to give away my Milky-white the best milker in the parish, and prime beef to boot, for a set of paltry beans? Take that! Take that! Take that! And as for your precious beans here they go out of the window. And now off with you to bed. Not a sip shall you drink, and not a bite shall you swallow this very night."

So Jack went upstairs to his little room in the attic, and sad and sorry he was, to be sure, as much for his mother's sake, as for the loss of his supper.

At last he dropped off to sleep.

When he woke up, the room looked so funny. The sun was shining into part of it, and yet all the rest was quite dark and shady. So Jack jumped up and dressed himself and went to the window. And what do you think he saw? Why, the beans his mother had thrown out of the window into the garden had sprung up into a big beanstalk which went up and up and up till it reached the sky. So the man had spoken the truth after all.

The beanstalk grew up quite close past Jack's window, so all he had to do was to open it and give a jump on to the beanstalk which ran up just like a big ladder. So Jack climbed, and he climbed and he climbed and he climbed and he climbed and he climbed and he climbed till at last he reached the sky.

And when he got there he found a long broad road going as straight as a dart. So he walked along and he walked along and he walked along till he came to a great big tall house.

On the doorstep there was a great big tall woman.

"Good morning, mum," says Jack, quite polite-like. "Could you be so kind as to give me some breakfast?" For he hadn't had anything to eat, you know, the night before and was as hungry as a hunter.

"It's breakfast you want, is it?" says the great big tall woman, "it's breakfast you'll *be* if you don't move off from here. My man is an ogre and there's nothing he likes better than boys broiled on toast. You'd better be moving on or he'll soon be coming."

"Oh! please, mum, do give me something to eat, mum. I've had nothing to eat since yesterday morning, really and truly, mum," says Jack. "I may as well be broiled as die of hunger."

Well, the ogre's wife was not half so bad after all. So she took Jack into the kitchen, and gave him a chunk of bread and cheese and a jug of milk. But Jack hadn't half finished these when thump! thump! thump! the whole house began to tremble with the noise of someone coming.

"Goodness gracious me! It's my old man," said the ogre's wife. "What on earth shall I do? Come along quick and jump in here." And she bundled Jack into the oven just as the ogre came in.

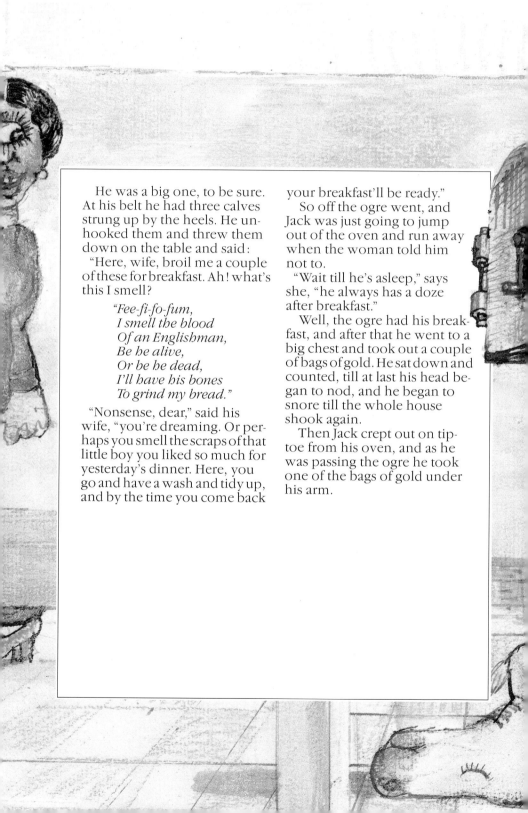

He was a big one, to be sure. At his belt he had three calves strung up by the heels. He unhooked them and threw them down on the table and said:

"Here, wife, broil me a couple of these for breakfast. Ah! what's this I smell?

> *"Fee-fi-fo-fum,*
> *I smell the blood*
> *Of an Englishman,*
> *Be he alive,*
> *Or be he dead,*
> *I'll have his bones*
> *To grind my bread."*

"Nonsense, dear," said his wife, "you're dreaming. Or perhaps you smell the scraps of that little boy you liked so much for yesterday's dinner. Here, you go and have a wash and tidy up, and by the time you come back your breakfast'll be ready."

So off the ogre went, and Jack was just going to jump out of the oven and run away when the woman told him not to.

"Wait till he's asleep," says she, "he always has a doze after breakfast."

Well, the ogre had his breakfast, and after that he went to a big chest and took out a couple of bags of gold. He sat down and counted, till at last his head began to nod, and he began to snore till the whole house shook again.

Then Jack crept out on tiptoe from his oven, and as he was passing the ogre he took one of the bags of gold under his arm.

Then off he ran till he came to the beanstalk. He threw down the bag of gold, which, of course, fell into his mother's garden. Then he climbed down and climbed down till at last he got home. He showed his mother the gold and said:

"Well, mother, wasn't I right about the beans? They really are magical, you see."

So they lived on the bag of gold for some time. But at last they came to the end of it, and Jack made up his mind to try his luck once more up at the top of the beanstalk. So one fine morning he rose up early, and got on to the beanstalk, and he climbed and he climbed and he climbed and he climbed and he climbed and he climbed till at last he came out on to the road again and up to the great big tall house he had been to before.

There, sure enough, was the great big tall woman standing on the doorstep.

"Good morning, mum," says Jack, as bold as brass. "Could you be so good as to give me something to eat?"

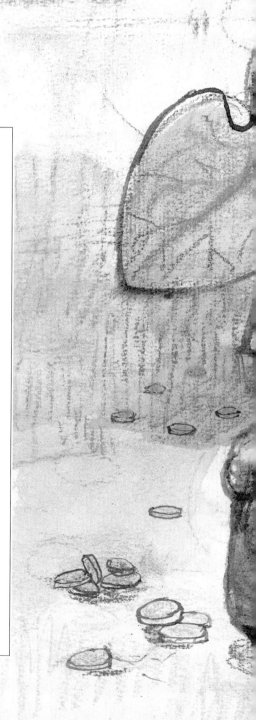

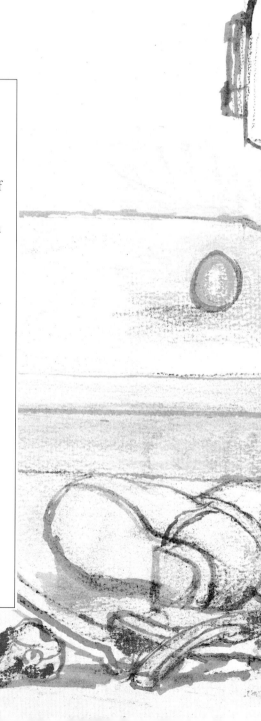

"Go away, my boy," said the big tall woman, "or else my man will eat you up for breakfast. But aren't you the youngster who came here once before? Do you know, that very day, my man missed one of his bags of gold."

"That's strange, mum," said Jack. "I dare say I could tell you something about that, but I'm so hungry I can't speak till I've had something to eat."

Well the big tall woman was so curious that she took him in and gave him something to eat. But he had scarcely begun munching, when thump! thump! thump! they heard the giant's footstep, and his wife hid Jack away in the oven.

All happened as it did before. In came the ogre as he did before. He said:

"Fee-fi-fo-fum," and had his breakfast of three broiled oxen.

Then he said:

"Wife, bring me the hen that lays the golden eggs."

So she brought it, and the ogre said: "Lay," and it laid an egg all of gold. And then the ogre began to nod his head and to snore till the house shook.

Then Jack crept out of the oven on tiptoe and caught hold of the golden hen, and was off before you could say "Jack Robinson." But this time the hen gave a cackle which woke the ogre, and just as Jack got out of the house he heard him calling:

"Wife, wife, what have you done with my golden hen?"

And the wife said:

"Why, my dear?"

But that was all Jack heard, for he rushed off to the bean-stalk and climbed down like a house on fire. And when he got home he showed his mother the wonderful hen, and said "Lay" to it. It laid a golden egg every time he said "Lay."

Well, Jack was not content, and it wasn't very long before he decided to have another try at his luck up at the top of the beanstalk. So one fine morning, he rose up early, and got on to the beanstalk. He climbed and he climbed and he climbed and he climbed till he got to the top. But this time he knew better than to go straight to the ogre's house. And when he got near it, he waited behind a bush till he saw the ogre's wife come out with a pail to get water and then he crept into the house and got into the copper. He hadn't been there long when he heard thump! thump! thump! as before, and in came the ogre and his wife.

"Fee-fi-fo-fum, I smell the blood of an Englishman," cried out the ogre. "I smell him, wife, I smell him."

"Do you, my dearie?" says the ogre's wife. "Then, if it's that little rogue that stole your gold and the hen that laid the golden eggs, he's sure to have gotten into the oven."

And they both rushed to the oven. But Jack wasn't there, luckily, and the ogre's wife said:

"There you are again with your fee-fi-fo-fum. Why, of course it's the boy you caught last night that I've just broiled for your breakfast. How forgetful I am, and how careless you are not to know the difference between live and dead after all these years."

So the ogre sat down to the breakfast and ate it, but every now and then he would mutter:

"Well, I could have sworn...."

Then he'd get up and search

the larder and the cupboards and everything, only, luckily, he didn't think of the copper.

After breakfast was over, the ogre called out:

"Wife, wife, bring me my golden harp."

So she brought it and put it on the table before him. Then he said: "Sing!" and the golden harp sang most beautifully. And it went on singing till the ogre fell asleep and began to snore like thunder.

Then Jack lifted up the copper-lid very quietly and got down like a mouse and crept on hands and knees till he came to the table. Then up he crawled, caught hold of the golden harp and dashed with it toward the door. But the harp called out quite loud: "Master! Master!" and the ogre woke up just in time to see Jack running off with his harp.

Jack ran as fast as he could, and the ogre came rushing after. He would soon have caught him, only Jack had a head start and dodged him a bit and knew where he was going. When he got to the beanstalk, the ogre was not more than twenty yards away. Then suddenly Jack disap-peared, and when the ogre came to the end of the road, he saw Jack climbing down the beanstalk for dear life. Well, the ogre didn't like trusting himself to such a delicate ladder, so he stood and waited. That gave Jack another head start.

But just then the harp cried out: "Master! Master!" and the ogre swung himself down on to the beanstalk, which shook with his weight. Down climbed Jack, and after him climbed the ogre.

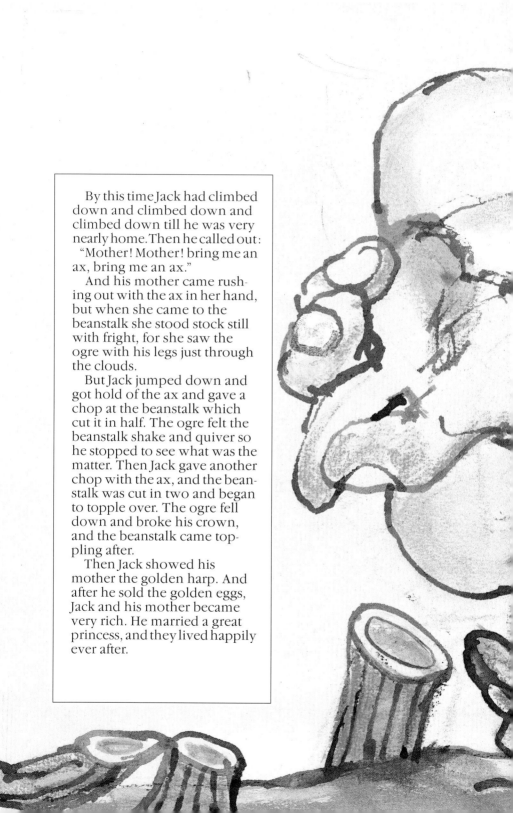

By this time Jack had climbed down and climbed down and climbed down till he was very nearly home. Then he called out:

"Mother! Mother! bring me an ax, bring me an ax."

And his mother came rushing out with the ax in her hand, but when she came to the beanstalk she stood stock still with fright, for she saw the ogre with his legs just through the clouds.

But Jack jumped down and got hold of the ax and gave a chop at the beanstalk which cut it in half. The ogre felt the beanstalk shake and quiver so he stopped to see what was the matter. Then Jack gave another chop with the ax, and the beanstalk was cut in two and began to topple over. The ogre fell down and broke his crown, and the beanstalk came toppling after.

Then Jack showed his mother the golden harp. And after he sold the golden eggs, Jack and his mother became very rich. He married a great princess, and they lived happily ever after.